Rachel Isadora

I HEAR

Greenwillow Books, New York

First Edition   1   2   3   4   5   6   7   8   9   10

Library of Congress Cataloging in Publication Data

Isadora, Rachel.
I hear.
Summary: A baby responds to all
the familiar things she hears.
[1. Babies—Fiction.
2. Hearing—Fiction]
I. Title.
PZ7.I763Iah 1985   [E]   84-6103
ISBN 0-688-04061-6
ISBN 0-688-04062-4 (lib. bdg.)

For Gillian Heather

I HEAR THE CLOCK.
TICK TOCK.

I HEAR FOOTSTEPS.
IT'S MOMMY
AND
DADDY.

I HEAR THE KETTLE
WHISTLE.
TIME FOR BREAKFAST.

I HEAR
THE VACUUM.
VROOM,
VROOM.

I HEAR MY CAT.
MEOW, MEOW.

I HEAR THE DUCKS.
QUACK, QUACK.

I HEAR AN AIRPLANE.
I LOOK UP.

I HEAR MUSIC.
I DANCE.

I HEAR THE RAIN.
SPLISH SPLASH.

I HEAR
THE DRAGON.
I ROAR.

I HEAR WATER.
BATHTIME.

I HEAR A STORY.
I LAUGH.

I HEAR A LULLABY.

GOOD NIGHT.